The Gross and Goofy Body

The Skin You're In!

The Secrets of Skin

By Melissa Stewart

Illustrated by Janet Hamlin

Marshall Cavendish Benchmark

New York

**THIS BOOK WAS MADE POSSIBLE,
IN PART, BY A GRANT FROM THE
SOCIETY OF CHILDREN'S BOOK WRITERS AND ILLUSTRATORS.**

Published by Marshall Cavendish Benchmark
An imprint of Marshall Cavendish Corporation

Other Marshall Cavendish Offices:
Marshall Cavendish International (Asia) Private Limited, 1 New Industrial Road, Singapore 536196 • Marshall Cavendish International (Thailand) Co Ltd. 253 Asoke, 12th Flr, Sukhumvit 21 Road, Klongtoey Nua, Wattana, Bangkok 10110, Thailand • Marshall Cavendish (Malaysia) Sdn Bhd, Times Subang, Lot 46,
Subang Hi-Tech Industrial Park, Batu Tiga, 40000 Shah Alam, Selangor Darul Ehsan, Malaysia

Marshall Cavendish is a trademark of Times Publishing Limited

All websites were available and accurate when this book was sent to press.

Library of Congress Cataloging-in-Publication Data
Stewart, Melissa.
The skin you're in : the secrets of skin / by Melissa Stewart.
p. cm. — (The gross and goofy body)
Summary: "Provides comprehensive information on the role skin plays in the body science of humans and animals"--Provided by the publisher.
Includes index.
ISBN 978-0-7614-4169-4
1. Skin — Juvenile literature. 2. Body covering (Anatomy) — Juvenile literature. I. Title.
QL941.S74 2009
591.47—dc22
2008033620

Editor: Joy Bean
Publisher: Michelle Bisson
Art Director: Anahid Hamparian
Series Designer: Daniel Roode

Photo research by Tracey Engel
Cover photo: Mel Yates/Stone/Getty Images

The photographs in this book are used by permission and through the courtesy of:
Alamy: John Miller, 10; Hugh Threlfall, 13 (top); worldthroughthelens-medical, 19 (right); Tina Manley/Central America, 20; Catchlight Visual Services, 23 (bottom); Digital Vision, 26; Photodisc, 31 (top); Jason Kwan, 31 (bottom); Simon Lord, 35; MedicalRF.com, 37 (top). *Corbis*: Pat Doyle, 33 (bottom). *Getty Images*: George Grall/National Geographic, 5 (top); Jim Merli/Visuals Unlimited, 7 (top); Charlie Roy/Workbook Stock, 8; Altrendo Images, 9 (bottom); Jose Luis Pelaez/Iconica, 11 (top); Walter B. McKenzie/Stone, 11 (bottom); Chris Carroll/UpperCut Images, 12; Bernhard Lang/Riser, 14; Dennie Cody/Taxi, 15 (bottom); Andreas Kuehn/Taxi, 17; 3D4Medical.com, 18, 25 (top); Alex Kerstitch/ Visuals Unlimited, 21 (top); Joe McDonald/Visuals Unlimted, 21 (bottom); John Giustina/Iconica, 25 (bottom); Beth Dixson/Photonica, 27; Bob Elsdale/The Image Bank, 29 (top); Charles C. Place/Stone, 29 (bottom); Tara Moore/Stone, 30; Michael Najjar/Photonica, 32; Camille Tokerud/Photographer's Choice, 34 (left); Loungepark/Taxi, 38 (right); Ebby May/Taxi, 39; Thomas Kitchin & Victoria Hurst/All Canada Photos, 41 (right). *Minden Pictures*: D. Parer & E. Parer-Cook 7 (bottom). *Photo Researchers, Inc.*: Dr. P. Marazzi, 13 (bottom); Andrew Paul Leonard, 22; Edward Kinsman, 23 (top). *Shutterstock*: Luis Fernando Curci Chavier, 5 (bottom); Sharon Morris, 33 (bottom). *Visuals Unlimited, Inc.*: Dennis Kunkel Microscopy, Inc., 6.

Printed in Malaysia (T)
135642

CONTENTS

THE SKIN YOU'RE IN

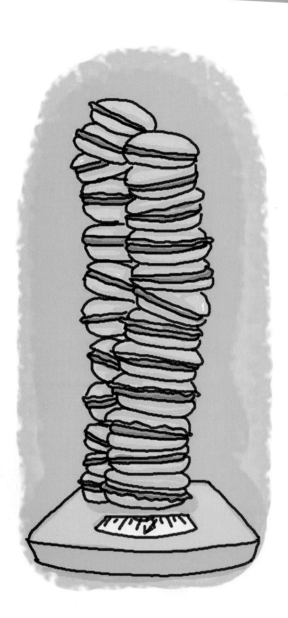

What's the first thing you notice when you look in a mirror? Your eyes? Your hair? Maybe your mouth?

What you probably don't notice is the amazing **organ** that covers most of your face—and the rest of your body, too. It's your skin.

Your skin is your body's largest and heaviest organ. It's big enough to drape over a twin-size bed, and it weighs as much as two dozen hamburgers.

In most places your skin isn't much thicker than a nickel, but you couldn't live without it. You'll be amazed at all the ways skin makes life better for you—and for other animals, too.

Frogs and salamanders can breathe through their thin skin.

A polar bear has white fur, but its skin is black. Dark colors soak up heat from the sun more quickly than light colors, so black skin helps a polar bear stay warm in its cold Arctic home.

When an anole lizard rests on a leaf, its green skin makes it hard to spot. But when the little lizard moves onto a tree trunk, its skin slowly darkens to match its new surroundings.

GOING, GOING, GONE

Human skin as seen under a microscope.

Gently run your fingertip along the furrows and folds on the sides of your nose. It won't take long for a milky white wad to build up underneath your fingernail. Scrape it out and take a closer look.

What you'll see is a mangled mash of dead skin cells—thousands of them. But don't worry, it's no big deal.

Your **epidermis**—the outermost part of your skin—loses about 50,000 dead skin cells every minute. That adds up to about 3 million cells every hour. No wonder dead skin is the main ingredient in household dust!

Some skin cells fall off when they rub against your clothes. More wash off when you take a bath. A month from now a whole new epidermis will cover your body.

Quick Change

Your epidermis flakes off a little at a time, but some animals lose theirs all at once.

A snake outgrows its epidermis three or four times a year. When the old skin starts to split open, the snake crawls forward. Its epidermis usually peels off in one long piece.

Some frogs shed their epidermis every week. They stretch out their old skin and pull it over their head. Then they eat it. Mmmm! Delicious!

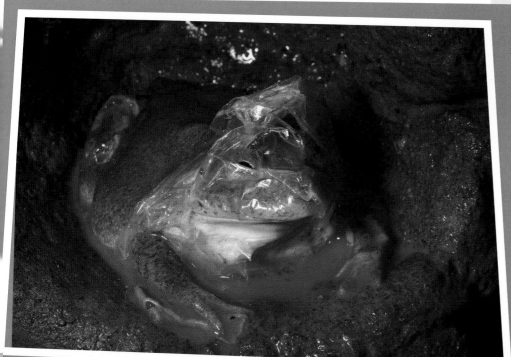

INSIDE YOUR EPIDERMIS

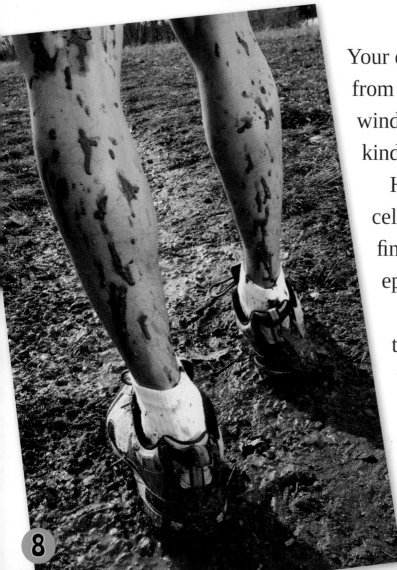

Your epidermis protects your body from the outside world. It keeps out wind and water, dirt and dust, and all kinds of nasty **germs**.

How can a bunch of dead, flaky cells do such an important job? To find out, take a look inside your epidermis.

The hard, flat, dead cells at the top of your epidermis overlap like the shingles on a roof. Almost nothing gets past them. As the cells wear down and flake off, they're replaced by newer cells from below.

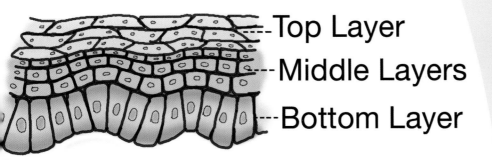

Top Layer
Middle Layers
Bottom Layer

Cells in the middle layers are slowly dying. But before they go kaput, they crank out as much **keratin** as they can. Tough and strong, keratin helps dead cells last longer before flaking off.

As the living cells at the bottom of your epidermis divide to create new cells, older cells move up toward the surface of your skin.

When Skin Fights Back

What do video games and violins have in common? Play them too much or too long, and the sensitive skin on your fingertips won't be able to take the pressure. To protect itself, your epidermis pumps out cells with an extra supply of superstrong keratin. Over time a thick, tough **callus** forms on the surface of your skin.

THE MAGIC OF MELANIN

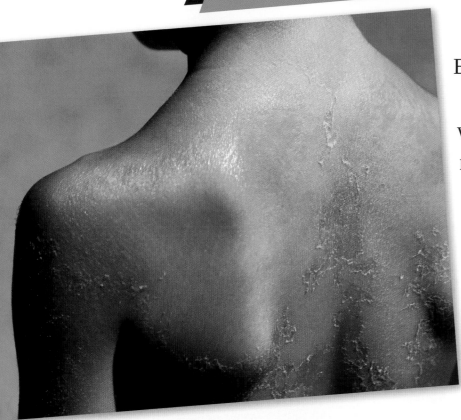

Ever had a sunburn? Ouch! But consider this: It would have hurt a lot more if you didn't have **melanin** in your skin. Melanin is a **pigment**, a naturally colored material, that protects your body from the sun's harmful rays. It also gives your skin its color. When you spend just a little time in the sun, your epidermis makes extra melanin. Then you get a suntan, not a sunburn.

Some people are born with more melanin than others. If your skin is dark, your **ancestors** probably lived in a hot, sunny place such as Africa or Central America. If your skin is light, your ancestors probably lived in a cooler part of the world.

Some people are born with no melanin at all. They're called **albinos**. They have white skin, white hair, and pink eyes. Other animals can be albinos, too.

The first humans lived in Africa about 200,000 years ago. Their dark skin had lots of melanin to protect them from the sizzling sun. As people moved to cooler places, they didn't need as much melanin. Their skin got lighter and lighter.

LOTS OF SPOTS

Take a good long look at your skin. It isn't one solid color. It's covered with all kinds of spots and splotches. Good luck trying to count them all!

You've had some of those spots since the day you were born. Others are probably just a few days old. Either way, melanin may be to blame.

- Got light skin? Dozens of freckles probably stretch across your nose. Or maybe they cover your arms. Ever noticed that those small, flat dots get darker when you spend time in the sun? It's because some of your melanin-making cells go into overdrive.

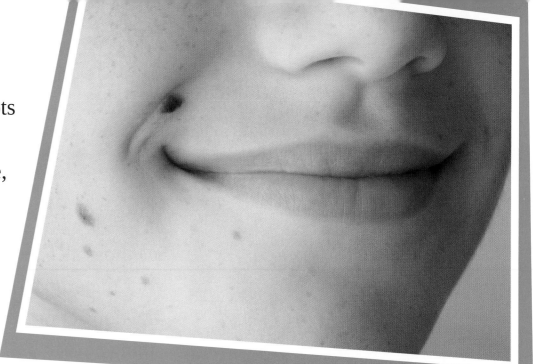

- Larger, darker dots called moles can show up anytime, anywhere, on anyone. They mark spots where melanin-making cells have clustered together. Whether they're raised or flat, moles usually get darker over time.

- Were you born with some patches of slightly darker skin? They're called café-au-lait spots. Like moles, they're caused by clumps of melanin-making cells. The spots often fade over time.

- Got dark skin? You were probably born with bluish black Mongolian spots on your back or your butt. But they should be gone by now. They're a sign that melanin-making cells are trapped deep inside the skin.

GET A GRIP!

See those swerving, swirling ridges on your fingertips? They give your skin traction action, so it's easier to pick up things.

There are three different patterns of finger ridges: looped, whorled, and arched. Which kind do you have? Make some fingerprints to find out.

1. Grab a white piece of paper and cover part of it with dark pencil marks.

2. Rub the tip of one finger on the shaded area.

3. Lay some transparent tape across your fingertip. Remove it gently and transfer your print to another piece of paper.

4. Repeat this process for your other fingers. Then compare your fingerprints to the samples on this page.

You also have rings of ridges on your feet and toes. They stop you from slipping and sliding.

Each ridge marks a spot where your skin's middle layer, the **dermis**, pokes up into your epidermis. The fingerlike bulges hold your dermis and epidermis together, making that skin strong.

Revealing Ridges

Everyone has a different pattern of finger ridges, so police can use fingerprints to catch crooks. Criminals have tried scrubbing their fingertips with sandpaper and burning them with acid. But when the wounds heal, the same pattern of ridges reappears.

BELOW THE SURFACE

To really understand the secrets of skin, you'd have to slice it open and take a closer look. What you'd see is all the tiny structures at work inside your dermis and **hypodermis**. They warm you up when it's cold and cool you down when it's hot. They keep your body moist, sense the world around you, and even heal wounds.

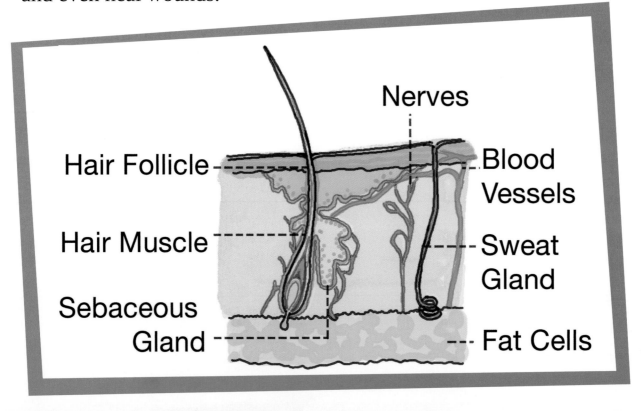

Here's what each part of your skin does:

- Each hair on your head and body grows out of a **hair follicle**.

- A hair muscle holds a strand of hair straight up when you feel cold or scared.

- A **sebaceous gland** makes oils that soften your skin and trap moisture inside your body.

- **Nerves** carry messages to and from your brain.

- **Blood vessels** carry blood to all the cells in your body.

- A **sweat gland** makes sweat to cool your body.

- Fat cells store fat and cushion your skin.

Full of Fibers

Your dermis is made of three kinds of fibers.

1. Tough, strong fibers hold your dermis together.

2. Durable fibers support all the tiny structures inside your dermis.

3. Stretchy fibers make your skin flexible. As people grow older, their skin wrinkles and sags because their stretchy fibers have trouble springing back into shape.

A FLOOD OF BLOOD

More than 11 miles (17.7 kilometers) of blood vessels crisscross your skin—and it's a good thing, too. Your skin needs a never-ending flood of blood to live and grow.

As blood flows through your skin, it drops off **nutrients** from the foods you eat. And it delivers plenty of **oxygen** from the air you breathe.

At the same time, blood picks up the vitamin D your skin makes. And it whisks away **carbon dioxide**—the waste material that forms when nutrients and oxygen mix together to produce energy for your skin cells.

As your blood continues its journey around your body, it delivers the vitamin D to your bones and **immune system**. And it dumps the carbon dioxide in your lungs, so you can breathe it out.

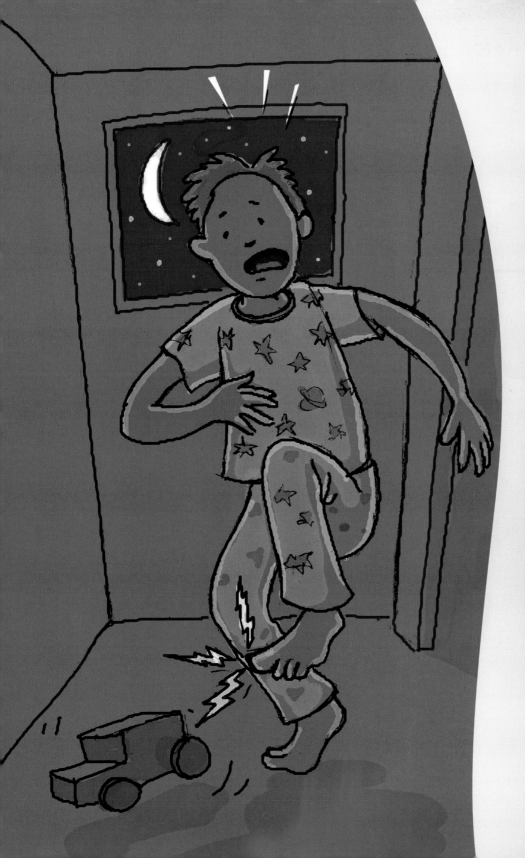

Bump and Break

You're headed for the bathroom late at night when—*thwack!*—you stub your toe. Yow, that hurts!

The next morning you see a nasty **bruise**. It's a sign that blood vessels deep inside your dermis broke open, and blood leaked out. As the area heals, you'll see some colorful changes— red, purple, black, blue, even a gruesome greenish yellow. Finally, the bruise fades away.

ON YOUR MARK

Ever been kissed by an angel? How about bitten by a stork? Of course not! But you might have been born with marks that made it look like you were. Ask your parents.

Angel kisses and stork bites are names given to birthmarks that quickly fade away. They occur when blood vessels clump together at the top of the dermis. Stork bites form on the back of a baby's neck. Angel kisses appear on the forehead or eyelids.

Clustering blood vessels can also cause strawberry marks and port-wine stains. Strawberry marks are raised, lumpy birthmarks on the head, neck, or chest. They take a few years to disappear. Port-wine stains may last a lifetime. These flat, reddish purple birthmarks are most common on the head, neck, arms, and legs.

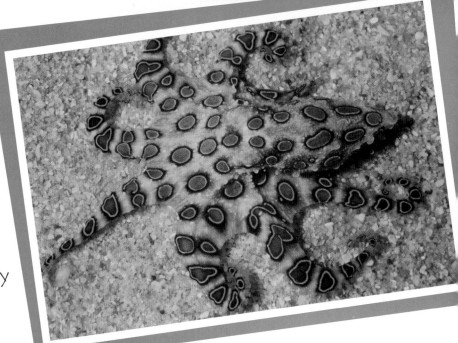

A blue-ringed octopus's body has enough poison to kill twenty people. Its colorful spots warn enemies to stay away.

The two large spots on a false-eyed frog's derriere scare away hungry hunters. They think the spots are the eyes of a much larger animal.

The speckles and spots on a chameleon's skin help the little lizard blend in with its surroundings.

21

SEAL AND HEAL

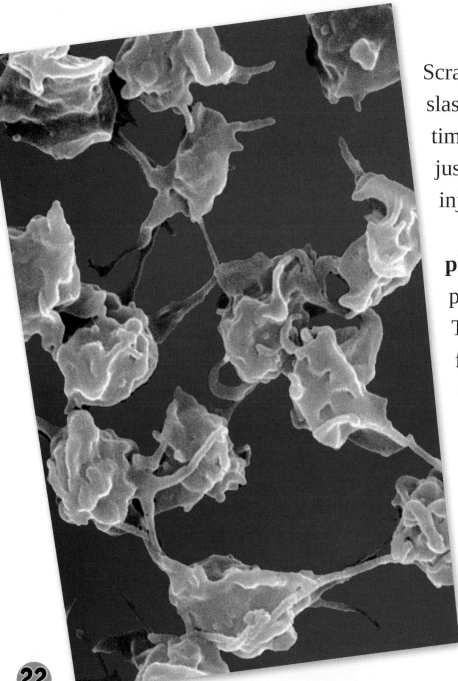

Scrapes and scratches, slices and slashes—you get them all the time. Luckily, your skin knows just what to do when it gets injured.

It doesn't take long for tiny **platelets** in your blood to pile up and plug your wound. Then a web of strong fibers forms. It traps blood cells, creating a **clot** that dries and hardens into a **scab**.

Next, your body's cleanup crew chases down dirt and **bacteria** that have snuck into the wound. Then it

Platelets are in charge of clotting action in your blood. This is what they look like under a microscope.

breaks down the damaged tissue and carts it away.

While nearby blood vessels stretch across the wound, cells in your epidermis divide faster than normal. The new cells slide under your scab to close the gap. Then tough, strong fibers in your dermis pull the edges of the wound together.

After about a week your scab falls off, revealing a brand-new layer of skin.

There's the Rub !

Wear your new sneakers too long, and you could be sorry. You might end up with a painful **blister** on your toe. As your skin rubs against the hard, new surface, your epidermis and dermis pull apart. The gap between them fills with fluid.

Feel like popping your blister? Don't do it! Cover it with a bandage and be patient. It won't take long for your skin to heal.

RED HOT

Ever told a joke, but nobody laughed? Ever been caught telling a lie?

When you're embarrassed or ashamed, a wave of heat spreads across your skin. You flush with a blush brighter than Rudolph's nose. But why?

Your feelings set off a chain reaction. Your brain tells your body to release chemicals. Those chemicals make your heart beat faster and pump more blood. Blood vessels all over your body open wide so the extra blood can flow through them. When the vessels in your dermis suddenly swell with blood, your skin turns red.

The same thing happens when your body gets too hot. Like dogs and ducks, eagles and elephants, you're a **warm-blooded** animal. Your body works hard to always stay the same temperature—about 98.6 degrees Fahrenheit (37 degrees Celsius).

When things heat up, your heart pumps extra blood to your skin. The heat escapes into the air, and your body cools off.

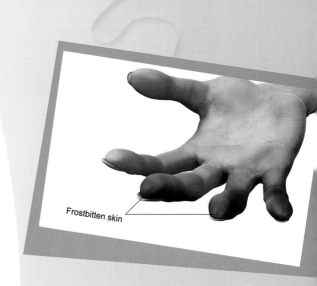

Frostbitten skin

Got a Chill?

When you feel cold, your heart pumps less blood to your skin. That helps you hold on to precious body heat. If your body gets really cold, blood vessels in your fingers and toes shut down. Then you can get frostbite.

DON'T SWEAT IT!

Your body has more than one way to keep itself cool. Besides blood, you depend on a clear, salty liquid called **sweat**.

Inside your dermis 2 million sweat glands are constantly cranking out a fresh supply of sweat. As your body heats up, the glands tighten. They squeeze drops of sweat onto your skin's surface.

Like the water slowly dripping out of a leaky faucet, your never-ending trickle of sweat really adds up. Most days your sweat glands produce enough sweat to fill a 1-liter soda bottle. On really hot days you churn out ten times as much. That's a lot of sweat!

Sweat can make your hands wet and clammy. And sometimes a few drops stream down your face. But most of your sweat **evaporates**. It turns into a gas and rises into the air—taking the heat in your skin along for the ride.

Drool That Cools

A dog can't sweat through its thick fur, so it cools off by panting. When the spit in a dog's mouth gets hot, it evaporates—just like sweat does. As the dog's tongue cools down, so does the blood inside it. Then the dog's heart pumps the cooled blood to the rest of its body.

PEE-EEEW!

WHAT STINKS?

Ever taken off your shoes and then nearly passed out? You probably thought sweat was the source of that stinking stench—but think again. Bacteria were to blame.

Bacteria love dark, damp places such as the insides of sweaty shoes. They feast on dead skin cells and oils from your skin. When they grow big enough, they split in half to produce even more bacteria. As bacteria multiply, they eat more and more food and produce more and more wastes. And those wastes really reek. That's what you smell when you take off your shoes.

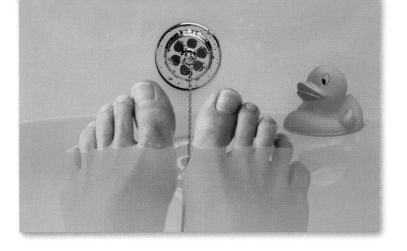

Don't want to sniff a whiff of foul feet? Wash your tootsies regularly with soap and water. Change your socks every day, and sprinkle some talcum powder in your shoes.

LOVE THOSE LOCKS

You wash them. You dry them. You brush and comb them, too.

You spend a lot of time taking care of the 100,000 hairs sticking out of your head. Luckily, you get a lot in return.

Your hair keeps you warm and protects your head from bangs and bumps. Not bad for a bunch of dead cells!

Like your epidermis, your hair is made of keratin. And melanin gives it color. Each hair sprouts from a follicle embedded deep in your skin. As living cells at the bottom of the follicle divide, the dead cells above them move up and out.

Your hair grows about 0.5 inches (1.2 centimeters) a month. At that rate it doesn't take long to grow a new eyelash or an eyebrow hair. The hairs in your scalp can keep on growing for seven years or more.

Hair, Hair Everywhere

Your head isn't the only part of your body that's covered with hair. More than 5 million short, thin strands grow on your arms and your legs and even on your back. Only three places don't have hair—your lips, the palms of your hands, and the bottoms of your feet.

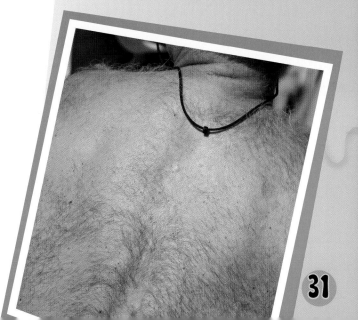

31

ITTY-BITTY BUMPS

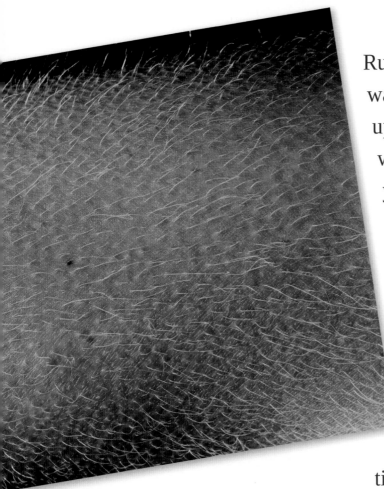

Rub a piece of ice on your wrist, and watch a wave of itty-bitty bumps spread up your arm. **Goose bumps** appear whenever you feel a chill—or when you're scared or excited.

After you warm up a bit, try that trick again. But this time watch the hair on your arms. It isn't just the little lumps that rise. Your body hairs do, too.

That's because each hair follicle on your arms, legs, back, chest, and belly is attached to a tiny muscle. When you feel cold, the muscle tightens, or contracts. And that makes your body hair—and the skin around it—pop up.

Since your body hair is short and thin, goose bumps don't do you much good. But imagine what they can do for animals with thick, furry coats.

When a rabbit is cold, fluffed-up fur traps a blanket of warm air close to its skin.

How can you tell when a chimp's stressed out? Just look at its fur. Upright means uptight.

When a cuddly kitty feels threatened, its fur sticks up straight. The scaredy-cat looks larger and fiercer, so enemies think twice about attacking.

DON'T SPOIL THAT OIL!

Stay in a pool or a bathtub too long, and the skin on your fingers wrinkles like raisins. That's because it's waterlogged.

Most of the time a thin layer of oily **sebum** coats your skin. It keeps your epidermis soft, smooth, and waterproof. That's why water usually runs off your skin when you wash your hands. Sebum also guards your skin against bacteria and **fungi**.

When you soak in water too long, all your sebum washes away. Water sneaks into your skin, causing those crumply crinkles.

What should you do to help your shriveled skin? Nothing! Your sebaceous glands will crank out a new coat of sebum in no time at all.

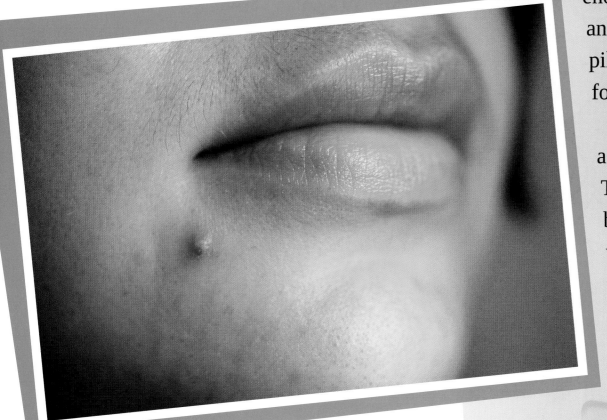

Oily Overload

You've probably never had a zit, but just wait a few years. Most teenagers get them. During **puberty**, sebaceous glands go into overdrive. And all that extra sebum can clog hair follicles. When enough oil and dirt and dead skin cells pile up, a zit will form.

Most zits have a dark center. They're called blackheads. But when bacteria get trapped inside, pus builds up and a zit becomes a whitehead.

WHAT A PAIN!

Your brother grabs you, puts you in a headlock, and rubs his knuckles back and forth across your scalp. Ouch! That's a noogie.

A noogie hurts because your skin is one giant sense organ. Your dermis is full of nerves that send messages to your brain. Nerves are long, stringy bundles of nerve cells. They run all through your body and

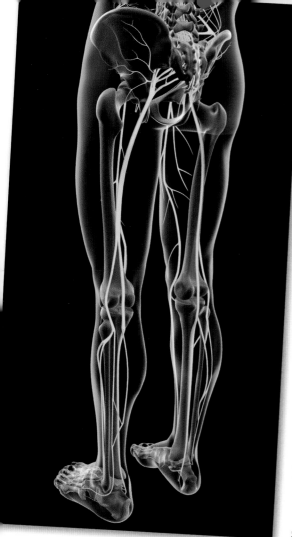

end in your skin. Most nerves are just a few inches long, but some stretch for more than 3 feet (0.9 meters).

Tiny sensors at the tips of your nerves pick up information from the outside world. The pain sensors in your scalp felt your brother's noogie. They can also detect pinches and punches, slaps and scratches.

Ditch That Itch

What does a scurrying spider have in common with a clothing tag? They can both make you itch. Scientists aren't sure how skin sensors detect an itch. But as soon as the message hits your brain, you start scratching. While your mind focuses on the mild pain of scuffing, scraping fingernails, blood rushes to the top of your epidermis. Soon the annoying itch fades away.

ALL SORTS OF SENSORS

You have at least four other kinds of sensors inside your skin.

• Hot sensors go to work if you touch a stove.

• Cold sensors send out messages when you touch an ice cube.

• Pressure sensors let you know when you're getting a hug.

• Touch sensors tell you that a sock is softer than a rock.

Some parts of your skin have more touch sensors than others. Want to find out which areas are most sensitive? Grab a pair of tweezers, and gently press the tips on different parts of your skin. Try your hands, face, arms, fingers, legs, feet, and toes. Have a friend test your back.

Now make a list of the places where you felt both tips. Those are your most sensitive spots.

The Fickle Tickle

You squirm and squeal when your mom wiggles her fingers across your ribs. But have you ever noticed that you can't tickle yourself? Blame your brain. The touch sensors in your skin send out messages no matter who does the tickling. But if your brain knows what's coming, it doesn't react.

SKIN TO THE RESCUE!

It's the final quarter of the big soccer game, and you're running out of steam. Suddenly, someone kicks you the ball. You look down the field, and the goal is open. Your mind says, "Go for it!"

A burst of energy rushes through your body. You race down the field and kick with all your strength. Score!

Where did that extra energy come from? Your hypodermis. It stores fats—one of your body's main sources of energy—and releases them into your blood when you really need them.

The fat in your hypodermis also keeps you warm by trapping heat inside your body. And it cushions your inner organs from bumps and knocks.

From protecting inner organs and keeping our bodies warm to sensing the world and healing wounds, it's hard to believe all the ways skin helps us every day. And we aren't alone. Other animals depend on it, too.

A Mat of Fat

What do whales and walruses, dolphins and seals all have in common? An extra-thick, extra-fatty hypodermis. Most people call it blubber. Blubber helps protect these warm-blooded animals from chilly ocean water.

GLOSSARY

albino—An animal without any melanin in its body.

ancestor—A person who lived before you and from whom you are descended.

bacterium (pl. bacteria)—A tiny, one-celled living thing that reproduces by dividing. Some bacteria can make people sick.

blister—A raised bubble of skin caused by rubbing. The dermis and epidermis separate, and fluid fills the gap between the two layers.

blood vessel—One of the tubes that carries blood throughout the body.

bruise—A mark on the skin that forms when blood vessels break within or below the dermis.

callus—A thick, hard area of skin that forms in response to repeated pressure.

carbon dioxide—An invisible gas that animals make as they get energy from food.

clot—A mass or lump. A blood clot is a mass of blood cells that plugs up a wound. It dries into a scab.

dermis—The middle layer of skin. It contains blood vessels, hair follicles, sweat glands, sebaceous glands, and nerve receptors.

epidermis—The top layer of skin. The uppermost part of the epidermis is made of dead cells.

evaporate—To change from a liquid to a gas.

fungus (pl. fungi)—A living thing made of many cells that is neither a plant nor an animal. Mushrooms and yeast are fungi. Some kinds of fungi can make people sick.

germ—A tiny organism or particle that can make people sick.

goose bump—A lump that forms on the skin when a hair muscle contracts, pulling up a strand of hair.

hair follicle—The tube from which a hair strand grows.

hypodermis—The bottom layer of skin. It contains a lot of fat cells.

immune system—A group of cells, tissues, and organs that fight germs and other invaders.

keratin—The main ingredient in dead cells in the epidermis.

melanin—The pigment that gives skin, hair, and eyes their color.

nerve—A cell that carries messages to and from the brain.

nutrient—A substance that keeps the body healthy. It comes from food.

organ—A body part made up of several kinds of tissue that work together. The skin is an organ. So are the heart, lungs, and brain.

oxygen—An invisible gas that animals need to live.

pigment—A naturally colored material.

platelet—A tiny cell fragment in the blood that helps close up cuts.

puberty—The period of a person's life when he or she goes through many body changes and becomes an adult.

scab—The dried remains of a blood clot. It acts as a protective covering until a wound heals.

sebaceous gland—A small sac that produces and releases sebum onto the surface of the skin.

sebum—The oil that keeps skin soft, moist, and a little bit waterproof.

sweat—A salty liquid that the body releases to help people and some other animals cool down.

sweat gland—A small sac that produces and releases sweat onto the surface of the skin.

warm-blooded—Having a body temperature that stays the same no matter how cold or warm an animal's surroundings are.

A NOTE ON SOURCES

Dear Readers,

By now, all the kids in my life know that I'm working on a series of books called The Gross and Goofy Body. It's thanks to their interest and suggestions that this book contains so much great information.

I had a long conversation about snake skins with a third grader from Lowell, Massachusetts, and a boy I tutor reminded me that polar bears have black skin. Not long ago, a friend's child asked me why his fingers were wrinkly after a bath. And my nephew insisted that I include noogies.

But I didn't steal all the ideas in this book from kids I know. I learned about the sublayers of the epidermis from medical textbooks. Articles in scientific journals taught me that blubber and the hypodermis are the same thing. These sources also discussed scientists' current theories about tickling and itching, and they explained what skin is made of. I found information about fingerprints and why our feet stink in popular science magazines.

The human body statistics came from a variety of sources, but because they were usually based on adult-size bodies, a doctor helped me convert them into numbers that are just right for the kids reading this book.

—Melissa Stewart

FIND OUT MORE

BOOKS

Green, Jen. *Skin, Hair and Hygiene*. Corona, CA: Stargazer Books, 2005.

Kee, Lisa Morris, and Ken Landmark. *Whose Skin Is This?: A Look at Animal Skin—Scaly, Furry, and Prickly*. Minneapolis, MN: Picture Window Books, 2007.

Seuling, Barbara. *Your Skin Weighs More Than Your Brain: And Other Freaky Facts About Your Skin, Skeleton, and Other Body Parts*. Minneapolis, MN: Picture Window Books, 2007.

WEBSITES

Kids Health

This site answers just about any question you might have about your body and keeping it healthy.

http://kidshealth.org/kid/

Layers of the Skin

This site contains great diagrams of and information about skin.

http://training.seer.cancer.gov/melanoma/anatomy/layers.html

INDEX

Page numbers in **bold** are illustrations.

ABOUT THE AUTHOR

Melissa Stewart has written everything from board books for preschoolers to magazine articles for adults. She is the award-winning author of more than one hundred books for young readers. She serves on the board of advisors of the Society of Children's Book Writers and Illustrators and is a judge for the American Institute of Physics Children's Science Writing Award. Stewart earned a B.S. in biology from Union College and an M.A. in science journalism from New York University. She lives in Acton, Massachusetts, with her husband, Gerard. To learn more about Stewart, please visit her website: www.melissa-stewart.com.

ABOUT THE ILLUSTRATOR

Janet Hamlin has illustrated many children's books, games, newspapers, and even Harry Potter stuff. She is also a court artist. The Gross and Goofy Body is one of her all-time favorite series, and she now considers herself the factoid queen of bodily functions. She lives and draws in New York and loves it.

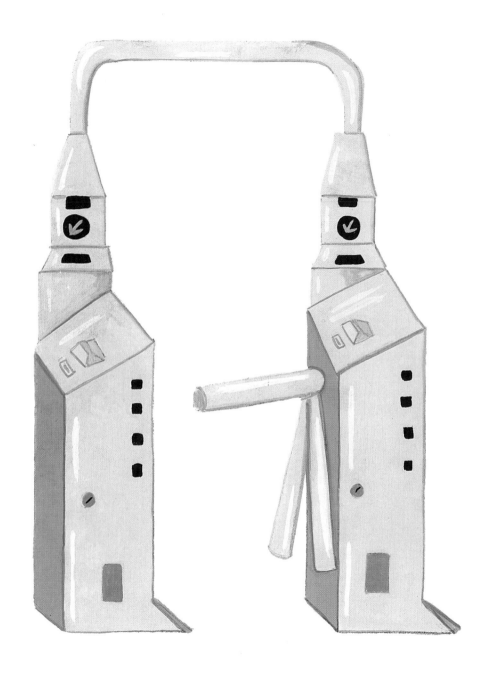

DOWN
in the
SUBWAY

story by
Miriam Cohen

pictures by
Melanie Hope
Greenberg

A DK INK BOOK
DK PUBLISHING, INC.

A Richard Jackson Book

DK Publishing, Inc., 95 Madison Avenue, New York, New York 10016
Visit us on the World Wide Web at http://www.dk.com

Library of Congress Cataloging-in-Publication Data
Cohen, Miriam.
Down in the subway / by Miriam Cohen; illustrated by Melanie Hope Greenberg—1st ed.
p. cm.
Summary: While riding on a hot subway train in New York City, Oscar and his family meet
the Island Lady and experience the sights, smells, tastes, and sounds of the Caribbean islands.
ISBN 0-7894-2510-6   [1. Subways—New York (State)—New York—Fiction.   2. Caribbean Area—Fiction.
3. New York (N.Y.)—Fiction.]   I. Greenberg, Melanie Hope, ill.   II. Title.
PZ7.C6628Dow 1998 [E]—dc21 97-43603 CIP AC

The illustrations for this book were painted using gouache.
The text of this book is set in 20 point Cantoria.
Printed and bound in U.S.A.

First Edition, 1998
10 9 8 7 6 5 4 3 2 1

Published in Canada in 1998 by Stoddart Kids, a division of Stoddart Publishing Co. Limited,
34 Lesmill Road, Toronto, Canada M3B 2T6

Distributed in Canada by General Distribution Services, 30 Lesmill Road, Toronto, Canada M3B 2T6

Tel (416) 445-3333   Fax (416) 445-5967   E-mail Customer.Service@ccmailgw.genpub.com

ISBN (Canada): 0-7737-3108-3
Information available from Cataloguing in Publication Data (Canada).

To my dearest Gladys, the Island Lady
—M.C.

To Shri Saraswati, the messenger dove
—M.H.G.

It was hot in that subway train. Ohhh, yes! Oscar twirled round and round the pole. Every time he came round, Oscar peeked at the Island Lady.

The Island Lady smiled a fine Islands smile.
"Would you like to know what's in this bag?"
Oscar looked at his mama. He was shy,
don't you see.
His mama smiled. "Yes."

Then the Island Lady reached down in her bag, and pulled out . . . the cool blue Island breeze!

"Please, what else is in that bag?"
said Oscar.
The Island Lady reached inside
and pulled out . . . the green
Caribbean Sea!

Oscar ran right in and splashed
and splashed.
Oh, my, he did enjoy that!

Next the Island Lady took out
the picnic lunch from her bag.
Ackee rice, salt fish, the callaloo,
and the soursop soup, guava,
pineapple, and the coconut tarts.
People on the train were just
looking at that food.
The fine smells,
don't you know.

"You must try it now, hear?" said the Island Lady. "There's plenty for all! Yes, indeed! Don't you stop eating now, child! Just leave some crumbs for the little lizards."

"Ummm," said Oscar, and he ate *another* honey-sweet tart. He couldn't help it, don't you see.

"Oh, listen, now! The Calypso Man is coming!"
the Lady said. "That man can make a song
about *anything*!"
Out of the Island Lady's bag jumped
the Calypso Man. He sang,

"Down in the subway.
Down in the subway,
Take the subway va-ca-tion!
Get on at the station,
Look at the people all smilin',
Takin' the trip to the Islands.

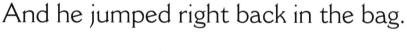

"Singin', 'Ackee rice, salt fish, callaloo,
Soursop soup, and the coconut too!'
Once again, mon! 'Ackee rice, salt fish, callaloo,
Soursop soup, and the coconut too!'"

The Calypso Man laughed.
And he jumped right back in the bag.

Now, don't you know, that
Island Lady's bag was wiggling
and bumping?
A whole steel band got
themselves out.

And didn't they play!
Those drums! Walking big like
thunder! And dance-y like little
raindrops on a tin roof.
The Lady was nodding her
head, tapping her toes,
and snapping her fingers.
"This is the jump-up music,"
she told Oscar. "Ohhh, yes!"

She reached in the bag, and pulled out . . . an Island town! And, don't you know, everybody in that town started doing the jump-up!

Well, all those people in the train got so tingly they just *had* to dance.

All the while, the subway train was racketing along the track, shaking with all that fine music and dancing.

"One Hundred Twenty-fifth Street station!" called the conductor. Now don't you know, that's just where Oscar and his mama and his baby brother had to get off.

The subway train pulled out of the station,
with the Island Lady, cool blue breezes,
green seas, callaloo, and soursop soup,
Calypso Man, steel band, little lizards,
and Island town.
"Good-bye, dear child, good-bye!"
waved the Island Lady.

After that, when Oscar and his mama
and his baby brother went on the subway,
they looked for the Island Lady's train.
But they never did see it again.

"Never mind, honey-sweetie," Oscar's mama said.
His papa said, "I *like* to hear you singing that song."
Well, don't you know, Oscar sang it so much,
pretty soon his baby brother could sing it too.